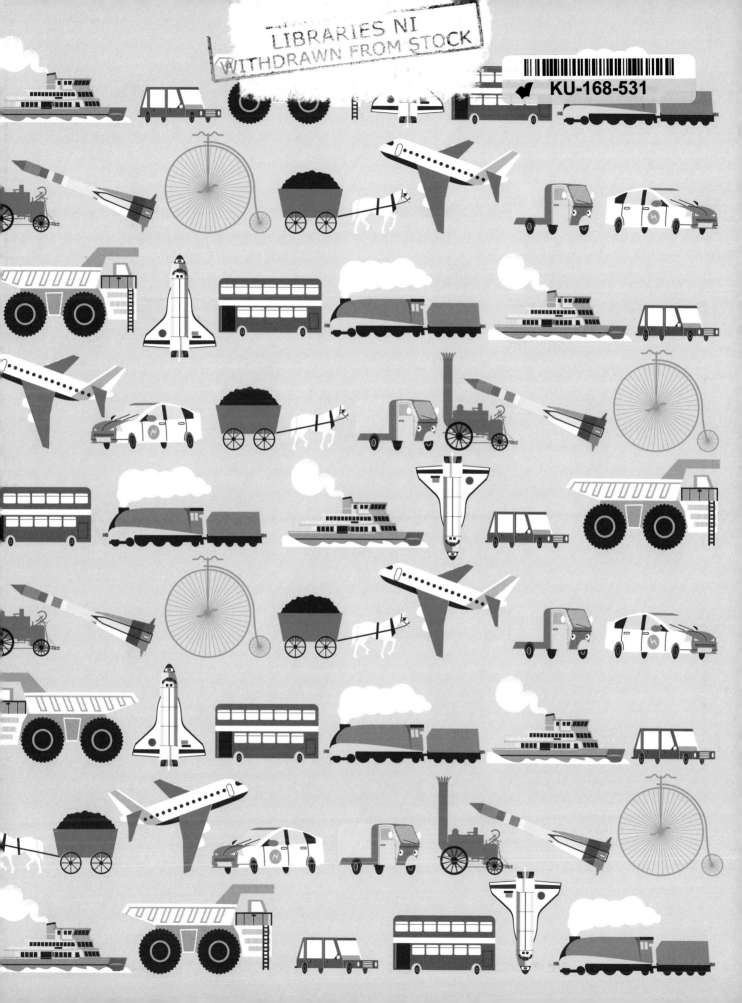

THE BIG COUNT DOWN

1.5 BILLION TRANSPORT VEHICLES IN THE WORLD

BEN HUBBARD

W

FRANKLIN WATTS
LONDON • SYDNEY

First published in Great Britain in 2018 by
The Watts Publishing Group
Copyright © The Watts Publishing
Group 2018

Editor: Julia Bird/Julia Adams
Design and illustration: Mark Ruffle
www.rufflebrothers.com

ISBN: 978 1 4451 6085 6

Photo credits: Bill Bachman/Alamy: 9br. Gerard
Bottino/Shutterstock: front cover c. Clashmaker/CC
Wikimedia Commons: 22b. Dryden Flight Research
Center/NASA: 11bl. Everett Historical/Shutterstock:
10bl, 13tr. Ina van Hateren/Dreamstime: 16b. Mariana
Ianovska/Shutterstock: 26b. Johnson /NASA: 7tl.
Corine van Kapel/Shutterstock: 19t.
Geof Kirby/Alamy: 18c. Steve Nicklas, NOS,NGS/
NOAA : 15b. Bart van Overbeeke/Alamy: 25b. Ruth
Peterkin/Dreamstime: 17b. Southern Metropolis Daily
2018/VCG/Getty Images: 21b. testing/Shutterstock:
24t. Thitisan/Shutterstock: front cover tr.

Franklin Watts
An imprint of
Hachette Children's Group
Part of The Watts Publishing Group
Carmelite House
50 Victoria Embankment
London EC4Y 0DZ

An Hachette UK Company
www.hachette.co.uk
www.franklinwatts.co.uk

Printed in Dubai

Throughout the book you are given data relating
to various pieces of information covering the topic.
The numbers will most likely be an estimation based
on research made over a period of time and in a
particular area. Some other research may reach
a different set of data, and all these figures may
change with time as new research and information is
gathered. The numbers provided within this book are
believed to be correct at the time of printing and have
been sourced from the following sites:

UN, Worldbank, Britannica, CIA Factbook, Economist
World Figures, World Health Organisation, The
Lancet, NASA, National Geographic, Britannica,
The Smithsonian, European Space Agency, World
Economic Forum, European Group on Museum
Statistics, Motion Picture Association of America,
National Geographic Society, National Oceanic and
Atmospheric Association, World Shipping Council,
Archaeological Institute of America, World Wildlife
Foundation, TIME magazine, Statistical Yearbook of
Mexican cinema.

FSC
www.fsc.org
MIX
Paper from
responsible sources
FSC® C104740

1.5 BILLION TRANSPORT VEHICLES IN THE WORLD

CONTENTS

COUNTING DOWN THE WORLD'S VEHICLES

We use around **1,500,000,000 transport vehicles** to move over land and water, and through air and space. These vehicles range from small, pedal-powered bikes that carry commuters to work, to massive cargo ships that haul thousands of containers across the world's oceans. The most common transport vehicle of all is the car.

CARS

Cars were invented around **130 years ago**. By 1900, less than **20,000 cars** were built worldwide. By 2016, this number had risen to **93,976,569**.

Only **0.2%** of cars produced today are electric. Other cars, powered by petrol and diesel, release carbon gas and polluting particles into the air.

Transport vehicles emit around **25%** of the world's carbon into the atmosphere.

Burning fossil fuels such as petrol releases carbon gas.

Petrol and diesel make up around **95%** of fuel used by transport vehicles.

BOATS AND SHIPS

The first boats were small canoes powered by oars. Today, over **50,000 ships** transport goods across vast shipping lanes that crisscross the globe.

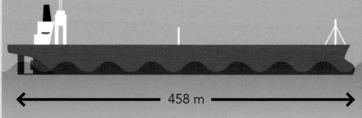

← 458 m →

Knock Nevis (see p.18), built in 1981, was the world's biggest supertanker. It was **458 m long** and could carry **646,642 tonnes** of weight.

The Pesse canoe is around **8,000 years old** and is the oldest boat ever discovered. It is **298 cm** long.

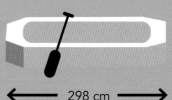

← 298 cm →

The two-man *Trieste* submarine (see p.14–15) descended to a depth of **10,916 m**: nearly the lowest point of the sea floor.

TRANSPORT TITANS

Trucks and trains carry goods, materials and people across land. Trucks are the largest land vehicles and are capable of lifting the heaviest loads. Trains carry billions of passengers every year over **1,051,839 km** of railway track worldwide.

Every year, over **1,600,000,000 passengers** around the world travel on high speed trains.

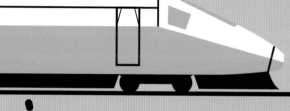

X 1,600,000,000

The longest truck, an Australian 'road train', was **1,474 m** long and towed **112** trailers. It was towed along a Queensland highway by John Atkinson in 2006.

X 112

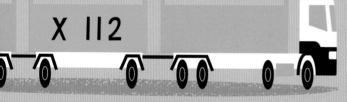

The BelAZ 75710 truck can transport a **450-tonne** load.

AIR AND SPACE

Humans first took to the air in 1783 aboard the world's first hot air balloon. Today, more than **4,000,000,000** people and over **50 million tonnes** of goods are transported by aeroplane every year.

HITTING THE HEIGHTS

HEIGHT IN KILOMETRES

700
600
500
400
300
200
100

HEIGHT IN METRES

24
20
16
12
8
4
0

1997: The Space Shuttle *Discovery* reaches the highest altitude of any space shuttle: **620 km**. In 2011, *Discovery* is retired after **39 missions** and a total of **238,539,663 km**.

2001: The Antonov AN-225 *Mriya* flies at an altitude of **10,750 m** carrying four tanks, which weigh a total of **253,820 kg**. It is the heaviest air load ever lifted.

1783: The Montgolfier brothers' first hot air balloon travels **eight km** across Paris, France, and reaches an altitude of **24 m**.

1903: The Wright brothers fly their *Flyer* for **12 seconds** across **36 m** of ground at an altitude of **2.4 m**.

Space shuttles were in use from 1981 until 2011. They carried people and cargo across the vast, dark distances of space. They took off like a rocket, and landed like a plane. Other spacecraft include satellites, probes sent to other planets and the Soyuz spacecraft, which travel to and from the International Space Station (ISS).

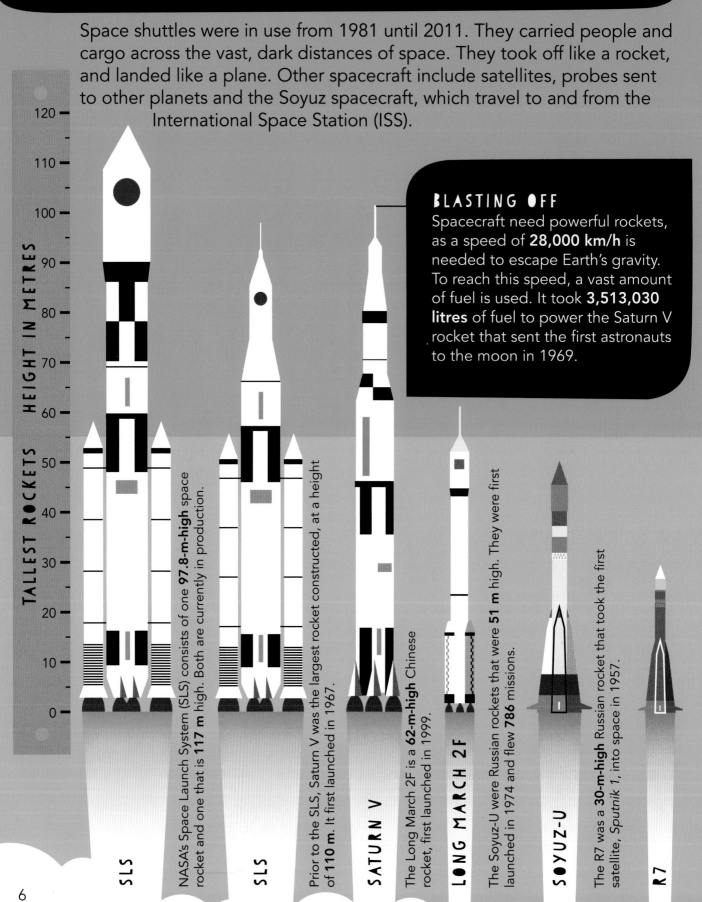

HEIGHT IN METRES

TALLEST ROCKETS

BLASTING OFF

Spacecraft need powerful rockets, as a speed of **28,000 km/h** is needed to escape Earth's gravity. To reach this speed, a vast amount of fuel is used. It took **3,513,030 litres** of fuel to power the Saturn V rocket that sent the first astronauts to the moon in 1969.

SLS

NASA's Space Launch System (SLS) consists of one **97.8-m-high** space rocket and one that is **117 m** high. Both are currently in production.

SLS

Prior to the SLS, Saturn V was the largest rocket constructed, at a height of **110 m**. It first launched in 1967.

SATURN V

The Long March 2F is a **62-m-high** Chinese rocket, first launched in 1999.

LONG MARCH 2F

The Soyuz-U were Russian rockets that were **51 m** high. They were first launched in 1974 and flew **786** missions.

SOYUZ-U

The R7 was a **30-m-high** Russian rocket that took the first satellite, Sputnik 1, into space in 1957.

R7

Astronauts from **17** different nations have taken turns living aboard the ISS, which is in orbit **354 km** above the Earth. The ISS is about the size of a football field and weighs **417,000 kg**. The astronauts perform experiments that teach us about the effects of living in space.

EARTH'S ORBIT

An orbit is the gravitational path an object takes around a planet or star. There are over **8,000** manmade objects in orbit around the Earth. One of these is the ISS. The ISS travels around the Earth at **27,600 km/h** and makes an orbit of the Earth every **92.65 minutes**. After its first **ten years**, the ISS had orbited the Earth 57,361 times: a distance of nearly **2,500,000,000 km**.

There are more than **29,000** pieces of space junk over **10 cm** in size circling the Earth.

SPACE TRANSPORTERS

The Space Shuttles and Soyuz spacecraft both transported supplies and people to and from the ISS. After the Space Shuttles were retired, the Soyuz spacecraft became the sole means of space transport.

SPACE SHUTTLE DISCOVERY

39 missions and **365 days** in space

Room for **10 crew**. Can remain in space for **28 days**

Made first docking with the ISS in 1999

Made **nine flights** to the ISS

Deployed the Hubble Space Telescope into orbit

SOYUZ SPACECRAFT

Room for **three** crew and life support for **30 days**

Made of **three parts**: the Orbital, Descent and Propulsion Modules

Takes around **six hours** from Earth to dock at the ISS

Over **40 years** in service

THERE ARE 1,051,839 KM OF RAILWAY TRACK IN THE WORLD

Trains are one of the most efficient and eco-friendly means of transport. There are different kinds of train, including steam, diesel and electric, but they all run on tracks. There are **1,051,839 km** of railway track worldwide. That's enough to wrap around the Earth **26 times**!

CIRCUMFERENCE OF THE EARTH: 40,070 KM

X 26

TIMING TRAINS

The first trains were dragged along tracks by people and horses. Around **200 years ago** a 'mechanical horse' was invented. This was a steam locomotive, powered by coal, which could tow carriages. Englishman George Stephenson built one of the first steam locomotives in 1829, called *Rocket*. It had a top speed of **45 km/h**. A century later, in 1938, the *Mallard* train reached the top speed for a steam locomotive of **202.6 km/h**.

To date, the fastest train is the Japanese LO-series maglev which reached **603 km/h** in 2015.

MALLARD

STEPHENSON'S ROCKET

KM/H

HORSE

LO MAGLEV

The world's fastest trains do not sit on tracks using wheels, but hover around **1–10 cm** above them using magnetic levitation (maglev). This reduces friction and allows the trains to travel at very high speeds. High-speed trains are powered by electricity, so they emit far less carbon dioxide into the atmosphere than cars and planes.

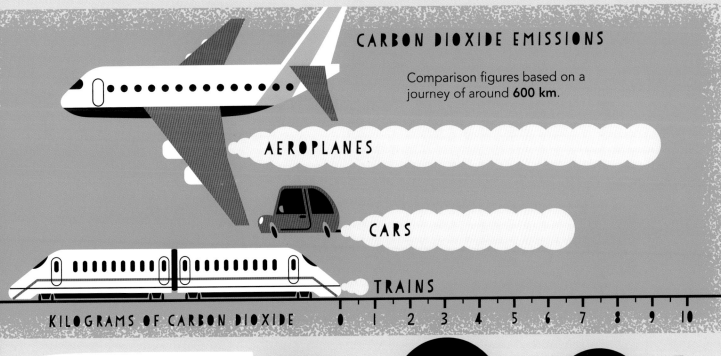

CARBON DIOXIDE EMISSIONS

Comparison figures based on a journey of around **600 km**.

AEROPLANES

CARS

TRAINS

KILOGRAMS OF CARBON DIOXIDE   0 1 2 3 4 5 6 7 8 9 10

TRACKING THE WORLD

Not all trains are high-speed passenger ones. Others carry freight over long distances. Trains in the USA carry the most freight annually at **2,547,253 tonnes**. Vast railway networks span the entire country and are used to transport farm produce, mined materials and cars.

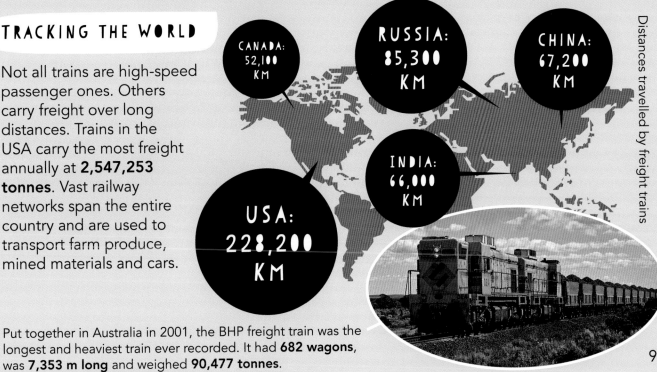

CANADA: 52,100 KM

RUSSIA: 85,300 KM

CHINA: 67,200 KM

INDIA: 66,000 KM

USA: 228,200 KM

Distances travelled by freight trains

Put together in Australia in 2001, the BHP freight train was the longest and heaviest train ever recorded. It had **682 wagons**, was **7,353 m long** and weighed **90,477 tonnes**.

9

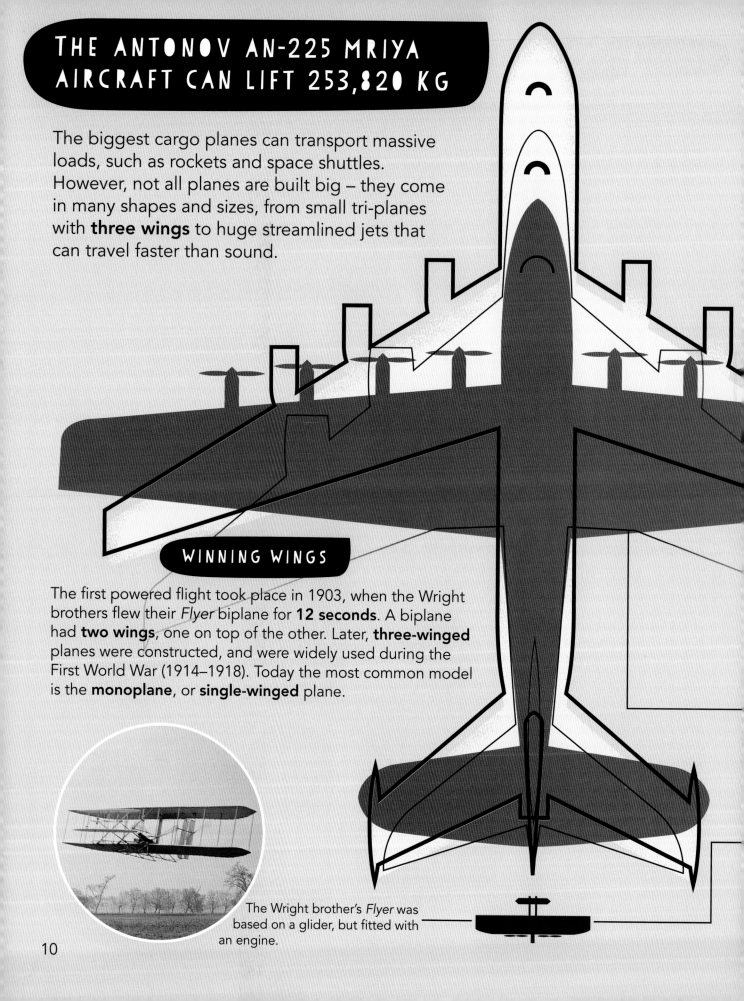

THE ANTONOV AN-225 MRIYA AIRCRAFT CAN LIFT 253,820 KG

The biggest cargo planes can transport massive loads, such as rockets and space shuttles. However, not all planes are built big – they come in many shapes and sizes, from small tri-planes with **three wings** to huge streamlined jets that can travel faster than sound.

WINNING WINGS

The first powered flight took place in 1903, when the Wright brothers flew their *Flyer* biplane for **12 seconds**. A biplane had **two wings**, one on top of the other. Later, **three-winged** planes were constructed, and were widely used during the First World War (1914–1918). Today the most common model is the **monoplane**, or **single-winged** plane.

The Wright brother's *Flyer* was based on a glider, but fitted with an engine.

BIG TO SMALL

There are many planes that are designed for specific jobs. They include some of the biggest and smallest fliers ever constructed:

THE H-4 SPRUCE GOOSE was built to carry military materials and men. It had the widest wingspan of any plane at **97.5 m**. The Goose had **four engines**, a crew of **three** and only **one** was ever built. It flew once.

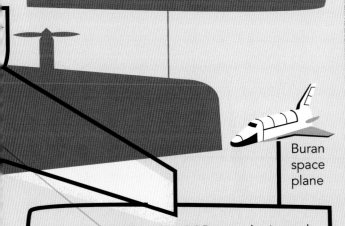

Buran space plane

THE ANTONOV AN-225 was designed to carry the Buran space plane. It holds the world record for the most weight transported by a plane: **253,820 kg**.

THE AIRBUS A380 is the largest passenger plane in the world. At **72.7 m**, it is as long as **two blue whales**. It has **two** passenger decks and can carry more than **540 people**.

THE FLYER had a crew of **one**, a wingspan of **12 m**, and a maximum takeoff weight of **274 kg**.

STAYING AIRBORNE

Planes have **four forces** that act upon them while they are airborne – lift, thrust, gravity and drag. A plane's engine thrusts it forward and its wings give it lift. These work against the force of gravity, which tries to pull the plane towards the ground, and drag, which slows it down. The lift and thrust have to be stronger than gravity and drag to keep the plane in the air.

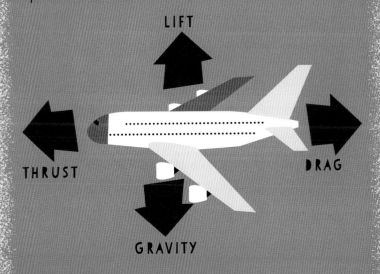

LIFT

THRUST

DRAG

GRAVITY

FASTER THAN SOUND

Most planes use jet engines to create thrust. These suck air into a fan and compress it so it shoots out of the back of the plane in a powerful jet. Some jet planes can travel at supersonic speeds. NASA's X-43A holds the record for the fastest speed in an aircraft at **Mach 9.6** (around **11,265 km/h**). That's **six times faster** than the speed of sound!

An illustration of NASA's record-breaking X-43A aircraft in flight.

THE HINDENBURG ZEPPELIN COULD HOLD 200,000 CUBIC M OF GAS

A zeppelin is another name for an airship. Hot air balloons and airships soar through the skies at speeds of over **115 km/h**. They use hot air or gas, such as helium, to stay airborne.

LIGHTER THAN AIR

The main part of a hot air balloon is called an envelope. It holds gas, and has an opening at the bottom. Underneath is a basket to carry passengers, as well as a 'burner' that injects a flame into the envelope's opening. This flame heats up the air inside the envelope. Because the heated air is lighter than the cold air outside, the balloon floats. The smallest hot air balloons contain around 600 cubic metres of air. Larger balloons have over 17,000 cubic metres.

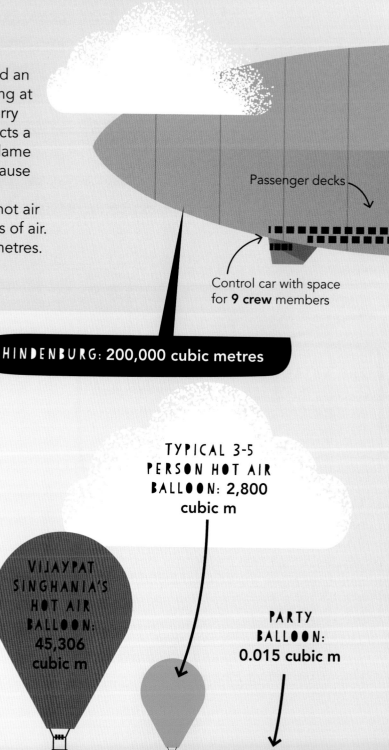

Passenger decks

Control car with space for **9 crew** members

HOW MUCH AIR?

HINDENBURG: 200,000 cubic metres

TYPICAL 3-5 PERSON HOT AIR BALLOON: 2,800 cubic m

VIRGIN PACIFIC FLYER: 74,000 cubic m

VIJAYPAT SINGHANIA'S HOT AIR BALLOON: 45,306 cubic m

PARTY BALLOON: 0.015 cubic m

BALLOON HEIGHT IN METRES

80 —
70 —
60 —
50 —
40 —
30 —
20 —
10 —
0 —

THE HINDENBURG

The German LZ 129 *Hindenburg* was the largest airship ever built. Throughout 1936, the *Hindenburg* carried **2,798 passengers** and **160 tonnes** of mail over **308,323 km** between Europe and the Americas. It met a tragic end in 1937 when it caught fire and crashed.

35 people died aboard the Hindenburg and **one** on the ground.

The *Hindenburg* was built with small, closed cells, each containing helium. If one cell burst, the others still contained enough gas to keep the *Hindenburg* in the air.

Ventilation valves

Metal frame gave the airship a stable shape

Propeller engines moved airship forwards or backwards

16 helium gas cells

HISTORICAL HEIGHTS

Hot air balloons were the first craft to enable people to fly. This chart shows some record-breaking hot air balloons.

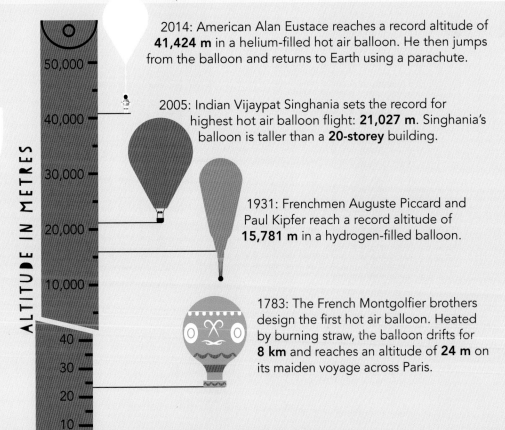

ALTITUDE IN METRES

50,000
40,000
30,000
20,000
10,000
40
30
20
10
0

2014: American Alan Eustace reaches a record altitude of **41,424 m** in a helium-filled hot air balloon. He then jumps from the balloon and returns to Earth using a parachute.

2005: Indian Vijaypat Singhania sets the record for highest hot air balloon flight: **21,027 m**. Singhania's balloon is taller than a **20-storey** building.

1931: Frenchmen Auguste Piccard and Paul Kipfer reach a record altitude of **15,781 m** in a hydrogen-filled balloon.

1783: The French Montgolfier brothers design the first hot air balloon. Heated by burning straw, the balloon drifts for **8 km** and reaches an altitude of **24 m** on its maiden voyage across Paris.

THE TRIESTE SUBMARINE DESCENDED TO A DEPTH OF 10,916 M

The record-breaking journey by the *Trieste* covered the greatest ocean depth reached by a human. To achieve this, the submarine travelled to the Mariana Trench's Challenger Deep, the deepest point on Earth's seabed at **10,898 m** below sea level. Here, the water pressure is so great that it could flatten a person instantly.

MOUNT EVEREST

The Mariana Trench is so deep that you could drop in Mount Everest and the distance to the surface would still be **two km**.

HOW SUBMARINES DIVE

Air is expelled from ballast tanks and filled with water when the submarine needs to dive.

Ballast tanks

Outer hull

Vent

Water is pumped from ballast tanks and filled with air when submarine needs to surface.

Modern submarines do not use pigskin bladders. But they use the same principle, pumping air and water in and out of ballast tanks.

FIRST SUBMARINE

The first submarine was built in 1620 by Dutchman Cornelius Drebbel. It could carry **16 passengers**, reach a depth of **4.5 m** and stay submerged for **three hours**. The submarine was a modified rowing boat with oars, covered in greased leather, and containing pigskin bladders. To dive, the bladders were opened to let water in. To resurface the water was squeezed out and replaced by air.

SEA DEPTH IN METRES

0
1000
2000
3000
4000
5000
6000

Submarines are often used in warfare. The largest military submarines are powered by **two nuclear reactors** and carry nuclear missiles onboard. Russia's Typhoon Class submarines are the biggest in the world. They are **175 m long, 12 m across,** and can reach a depth of **400 m**. A Typhoon carries a crew of **160** and can stay submerged for up to **120 days** at a time.

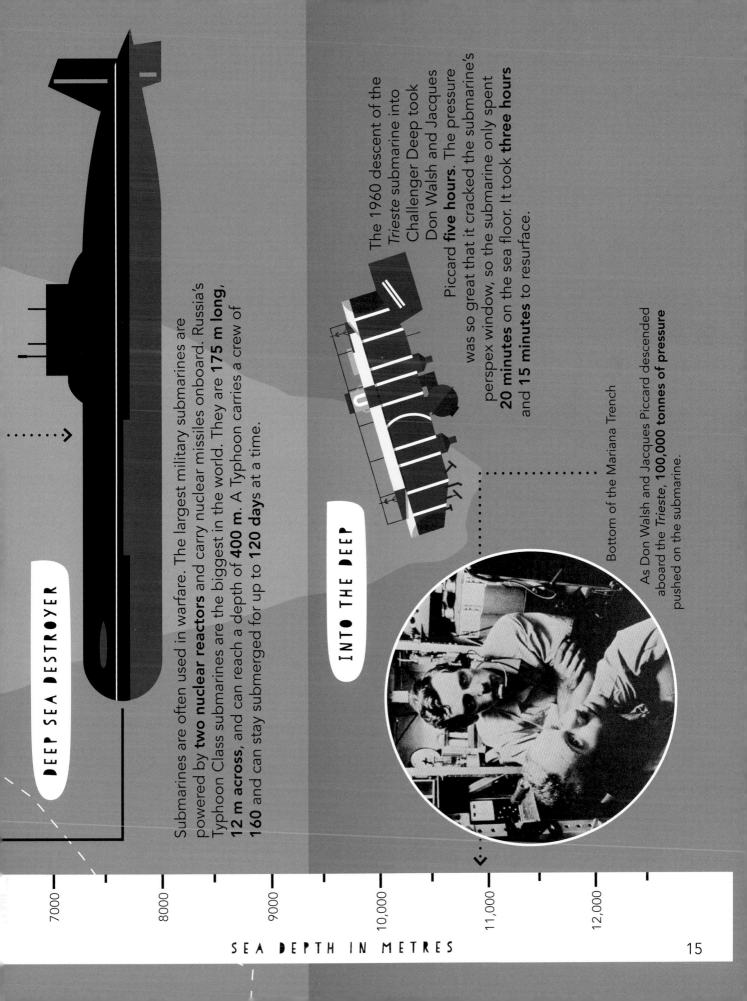

INTO THE DEEP

The 1960 descent of the *Trieste* submarine into Challenger Deep took Don Walsh and Jacques Piccard **five hours**. The pressure was so great that it cracked the submarine's perspex window, so the submarine only spent **20 minutes** on the sea floor. It took **three hours** and **15 minutes** to resurface.

Bottom of the Mariana Trench

As Don Walsh and Jacques Piccard descended aboard the *Trieste*, **100,000 tonnes of pressure** pushed on the submarine.

7000

8000

9000

10,000

11,000

12,000

SEA DEPTH IN METRES

15

Boats and ships carry goods and materials, as well as people. Passenger boats and ships range from small, **one-person** dinghies to vast cruise ships that carry thousands of people on holiday.

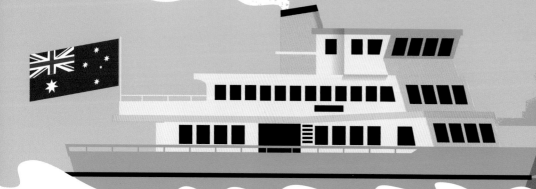

Over **15 million passengers** are transported by ferry around Sydney Harbour, Australia, each year.

HOW DOES IT FLOAT?

When an object is placed in water, it pushes aside – or displaces – some of that water. If the object weighs more than the water it displaces, it sinks. But as boats are hollow they weigh less than the water they displace. This means even very heavy ships can float. The heaviest cargo ship in the world, *Pioneering Spirit*, can displace up to **932,000 tonnes of water** with a full load.

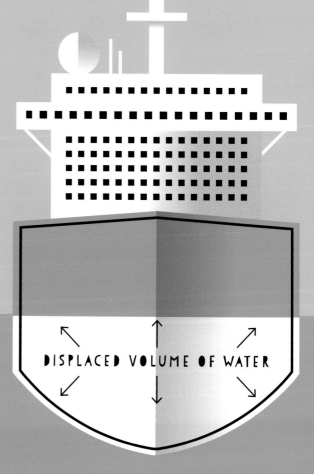

DISPLACED VOLUME OF WATER

Large docking cranes are needed to load goods aboard ships such as *Pioneering Spirit*.

LUXURY TRANSPORT

Large steamships first began transporting passengers and mail across the Atlantic Ocean in the early 1800s. By the end of the century, vast luxurious liners were built to carry people in style and comfort. The most famous of these ships was the RMS *Titanic*, built in 1912. *Titanic's* hull was constructed with **15 compartments** called bulkheads that were said to make her 'unsinkable'. But the ship did sink on 15 April 1912 after hitting an iceberg that tore into **six** of the bulkheads, almost instantly filling them with water.

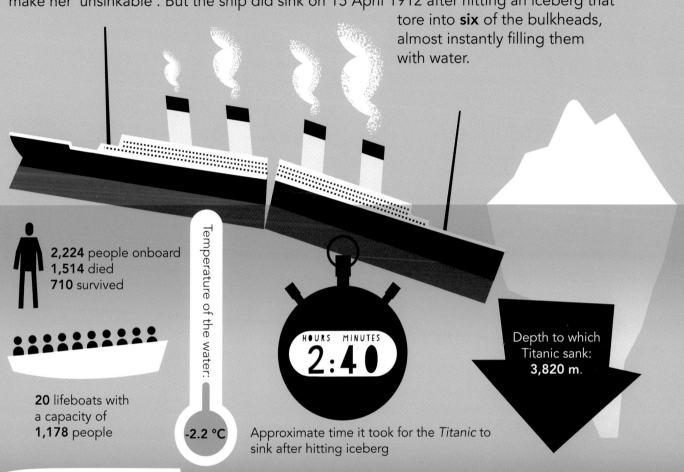

2,224 people onboard
1,514 died
710 survived

20 lifeboats with a capacity of **1,178** people

Temperature of the water: **-2.2 °C**

HOURS MINUTES
2:40
Approximate time it took for the *Titanic* to sink after hitting iceberg

Depth to which Titanic sank: **3,820 m**.

CRUISING TODAY

In 2017, over **25 million people** took a cruise ship holiday. Modern cruise ships are designed to give their passengers a luxurious trip. The ships normally travel around a body of water, such as the Caribbean Sea, and stop off at different ports so passengers can explore them for the day.

Large liners such as *Harmony of the Seas* can hold **6,780 passengers**.

COUNTING DOWN: MS HARMONY OF THE SEAS

1,400-seat theatre
20 dining rooms
10 hot tubs
9-hole miniature golf course
4 swimming pools
3-slide water park
2 rock-climbing walls
1 open air park

4,136 GREEK MERCHANT SHIPS

Greece has been transporting its goods across the Mediterranean Sea aboard merchant, or cargo, ships for **thousands of years**. Cargo ships carry goods and materials from one port to another. Today, there are over **50,000 cargo ships** in the world. Cargo ships carry more materials than any other form of transport.

SUPERTANKERS

The **two** biggest types of cargo ships are supertankers and container ships. Container ships carry goods inside large containers. Supertankers carry liquid cargo, such as oil. The largest supertanker was *Knock Nevis*. It could carry **646,642 tonnes** of weight. *Knock Nevis* was also the longest ship ever built at **458 m long**. This made it too large to sail through the English Channel, the Suez Canal or the Panama Canal – all major shipping lanes.

SHIPPING LANES

This map shows the world's shipping lanes crisscrossing the globe. Shipping lanes are the common trade routes used by ships to transport goods between ports. Over **80% of the world's goods** are transported by ship.

Knock Nevis was beached in India before being finally scrapped in 2009.

COMPARING SIZES

TITANIC 269 M

CUTTY SARK 65 M

DINGHY 2 M

CONTAINER SHIPS

The largest container ship in the world is the *OOCL Hong Kong*, which can carry over **21,143 twenty-foot equivalent units** (TEU). A TEU is the same as **one six-m-long** steel container – the containers commonly seen on ships and at ports. In 2016, around **1.7 billion tonnes of cargo** were transported by container ship.

OOCL Hong Kong being loaded with its enormous cargo

TOP FIVE MERCHANT FLEETS

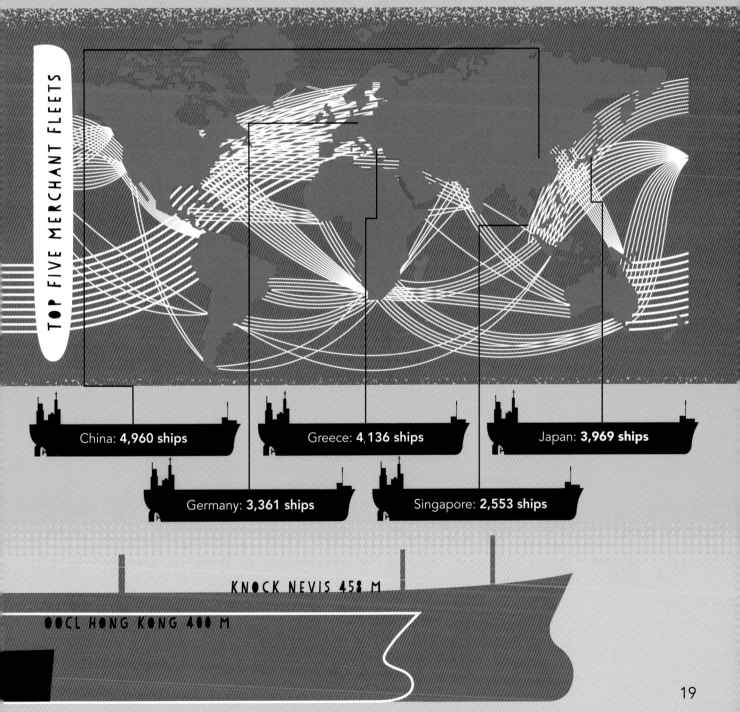

China: **4,960 ships**

Greece: **4,136 ships**

Japan: **3,969 ships**

Germany: **3,361 ships**

Singapore: **2,553 ships**

KNOCK NEVIS 458 M

OOCL HONG KONG 400 M

THE LAND SPEED RECORD SET BY THRUST SSC IS 1,228 KM/H

The first cars were unveiled to the world **130 years ago**. They were loud, uncomfortable and could only travel at around **16 km/h**. Today, cars are capable of speeds of over **400 km/h**.

THE FIRST CAR

German engineer Karl Benz built the first petrol-powered car in 1885. His **three-wheeled** Motorwagen only had **two forward gears** and reverse. The Motorwagen didn't sell widely until Benz's wife Bertha took it on a **194 km** joyride. This created so much publicity that by 1900 Benz had become the world's leading car manufacturer.

MOTORWAGEN: 16 KM/H

It took Bertha Benz **12 hours** to travel **100 km** in the Motorwagen. Today, **100 km** can be travelled in **13 minutes** in the Koenigsegg Agera RS car.

SNAIL: 0.001 KM/H

HUMAN: 44.64 KM/H

THE FASTEST CAR

The Koenigsegg Agera RS is the fastest production car ever made. In 2017, it broke records by going from **0 to 400 km/h** in under **34 seconds** and reaching a top speed of **447.19 km/h**.

MCLAREN-MERCEDES F1: 372.6 KM/H

KOENIGSEGG AGERA RS: 447.19 KM/H

JET-POWERED SPEED

Thrust SSC set the land speed record of **1,228 km/h** in 1997. To reach this speed, the Thrust SSC was powered by **two 9,000-kg jet engines** which normally power jet planes. The driver, Richard Noble, was also an experienced fighter pilot.

LENGTH: 16.5 M
WEIGHT: 10.6 TONNES

THRUST SSC:
1,228 KM/H

FIRST FLYING CARS

Scientists are now working on cars that can fly. The AeroMobil is a **two-person** vehicle with fold-out wings that can transform from car to plane in just **three minutes**. As a car, the AeroMobil can reach **160 km/h**, and **360 km/h** in the air. However, it also costs over **£1.2 million** to buy one!

Step 1: wings unfold from car

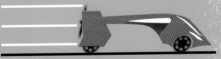

Step 2: takeoff speed of **144 km/h** reached

Step 3: car can fly for over **600 km** on **one** fuel tank

FLYING DRIVERLESS CARS

Driverless cars are expected to soon be widely used.
Experts say driverless flying cars will also become common. The EHANG 184 is like a flying taxi that can transport one person for a journey lasting about **30 minutes**. Its developers hope it will be in regular use by 2020.

Net weight: 200 kg
Charging time: 2-4 hours
Average speed: 100 km/h

The EHANG 184 driverless car can carry over **one person** over **500 m** into the air.

THE BELAZ 75710 TRUCK CAN TRANSPORT A 450-TONNE LOAD

There are two main types of truck – rigid and articulated. Rigid trucks are made from **one** single, straight chassis (frame). Articulated trucks are made of **two parts**: a unit at the front for the driver's cab and another part for trailers at the back.

DUMP TRUCKS

450 tonnes

x90

Some of the biggest trucks are used to carry earth and rocks away from mines. The BelAZ 75710 is the largest dump truck in the world and can carry a **450-tonne load** – the equivalent of **90 elephants**. The truck itself weighs a hefty **360 tonnes**.

4-m-high wheel x2

20.6 m long

x2

TRUCKING HIGHWAYS

One of the busiest highways for trucks in the world is Highway 401, in Ontario, Canada. The **828 km, 16-lane** highway has over **500,000** vehicles travel along it every day.

A busy highway such as Ontario's 401 is a trucker's worst nightmare!

TINY TRUCKS

The Piaggio Ape is one of the smallest trucks in the world. It was originally built in 1948 with a motorbike engine and **three wheels**. It is commonly used today to drive through narrow Italian city streets and as a roadside vegetable stall. It can only carry a load of **205 kg** – less than the weight of **three average men**.

Piaggio Ape

Length: **266 cm**

KEEP ON TRUCKING

IOWA 80
USA

is the biggest truck stop in the world. It has a **300-seat** restaurant, a cinema, a barber, a dentist and **450 employees**. It can park up to **800 trucks** and has served over **64 million** truck drivers since opening in 1965.

There are around **15.5 million trucks** in the US.

There are around **five million truck drivers** in India.

Argentina only produced **231,461 trucks** in 2016, compared with **1,604,294** by Mexico.

An average long-haul truck driver travels over **160,000 km** every year. That's **four times around** the Earth!

25% OF THE WORLD'S CO₂ EMISSIONS COME FROM VEHICLES

Carbon dioxide gas (CO_2) is released when fossil fuels such as coal and petrol are burned to create energy. Today, around **95%** of the world's transportation energy comes from petrol-based fuels.

Gas emissions from cars make up around **31% of the smog** hovering over Beijing, one of the most polluted cities in the world.

GREENER CARS

Electric cars are less harmful to the environment. Every year, sales of electric cars increase. In 2017, the number of electric cars worldwide reached over **2,000,000**. An electric car's battery can be powered at a home socket or at a public charging point. There are over **2.3 million** charging points worldwide.

Fast-charging stations can give some cars an **80% charge** within **30 minutes**.

ELECTRIC VERSUS PETROL

ELECTRIC:

Cost in electricity per km: 1-2 pence
Time to charge: 30 minutes to 8 hours (depending on charge type)
Range before recharge needed: 170 km
Gas emissions: zero

PETROL:

Cost in petrol per km: 5-8 pence
Time to fill tank: 2 minutes
Time to refuel: after 400 km
Gas emissions: 4.7 tonnes of carbon dioxide annually

THE FUTURE IS ELECTRIC

In 2017, **ten countries** agreed that by the year 2030 **30%** of the cars they produce would be electric. This would mean a total of around **140 million electric cars** on the road by 2030. In 2017, electric cars still only made up **0.2%** of all passenger vehicles worldwide.

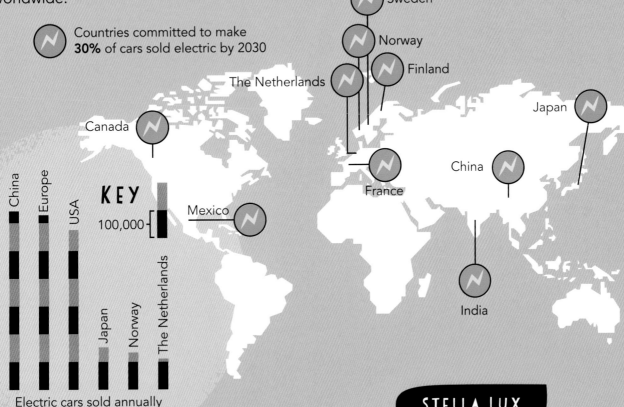

Countries committed to make **30%** of cars sold electric by 2030

Sweden

Norway

Finland

The Netherlands

Japan

Canada

China

France

Mexico

India

KEY

100,000

China
Europe
USA
Japan
Norway
The Netherlands

Electric cars sold annually

SOLAR-POWERED VEHICLES

Electric vehicles still need electricity to power them. This electricity is taken from central grids, which often generate electricity by burning a fossil fuel. Solar vehicles, however, power themselves through solar panels, using energy from the Sun. The Stella Lux, built by students from the Netherlands' Eindhoven University of Technology, won the competition for best solar car in 2013, 2015 and 2017.

STELLA LUX

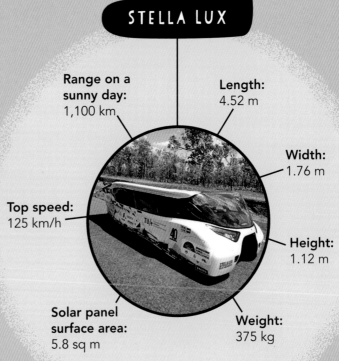

Range on a sunny day: 1,100 km

Length: 4.52 m

Width: 1.76 m

Top speed: 125 km/h

Height: 1.12 m

Solar panel surface area: 5.8 sq m

Weight: 375 kg

THE TOP SPEED OF NASA'S CRAWLER-TRANSPORTER IS 3.2 KM/H

The Crawler-Transporter belongs to an elite group of machines designed for the biggest jobs on the planet. These transport vehicles all have one thing in common: SIZE!

THE BAGGER 288

The Bagger 288 transports massive amounts of earth. It does this with **18 huge buckets** fitted onto a revolving wheel. The earth is then transported down the Bagger's conveyor belt and discarded on the other side. It can dig up **23,240,000 cubic m** of earth every day – enough to fill a hole the size of a football field **30 m** deep. At **96 m**, the Bagger 288 is the tallest land vehicle in the world.

The Bagger 288 dug the Tagebau Hambach coal mine in Germany in **six weeks.**

CRAWLER-TRANSPORTER

The Crawler-Transporter was built to carry rockets and space shuttles **5.6 km** from their hangers to the launch pad in Cape Canaveral. The Transporter also carries the launch platform: a **49-m-high** structure that weighs **3,730,000 kg** and sometimes has a **5,579,186 kg** launch tower on top of it.

A space shuttle adds another **5,000,000 kg** and the Crawler-Transporter itself weighs **3,000,000 kg.** Therefore the total weight shifted by a Crawler-Transporter can be a massive **17,309,186 kg.**

FUEL TANK

Weight

5,000,000 kg

75

70

65

60

55

50

45

Height in metres

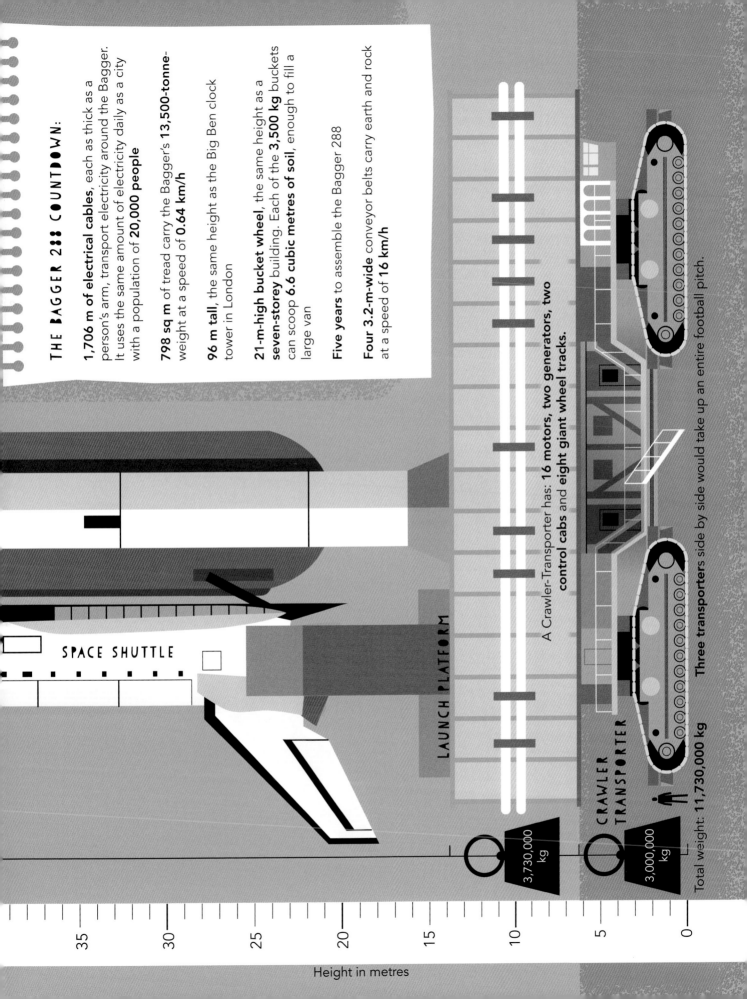

THE BAGGER 288 COUNTDOWN:

1,706 m of electrical cables, each as thick as a person's arm, transport electricity around the Bagger. It uses the same amount of electricity daily as a city with a population of **20,000 people**

798 sq m of tread carry the Bagger's **13,500-tonne-** weight at a speed of **0.64 km/h**

96 m tall, the same height as the Big Ben clock tower in London

21-m-high bucket wheel, the same height as a **seven-storey** building. Each of the **3,500 kg** buckets can scoop **6.6 cubic metres of soil,** enough to fill a large van

Five years to assemble the Bagger 288

Four 3.2-m-wide conveyor belts carry earth and rock at a speed of **16 km/h**

SPACE SHUTTLE

LAUNCH PLATFORM

A Crawler-Transporter has: **16 motors, two generators, two control cabs and eight giant wheel tracks.**

CRAWLER TRANSPORTER

3,730,000 kg

3,000,000 kg

Three transporters side by side would take up an entire football pitch.

Total weight: 11,730,000 kg

Height in metres

35
30
25
20
15
10
5
0

TWO WHEELS ON A BICYCLE

Although humans invented the wheel over **5,000 years ago**, bicycles are only around **200 years old.** However, they have never been so popular. There are estimated to be nearly **2,000,000,000 bicycles** in the world today.

EVOLUTION OF THE BIKE

1817 The German wooden Dandy Horse has a seat and handlebars, but is powered by the rider pushing their feet along the ground. It can reach a speed of **15 km/h.**

1872 The British Penny Farthing attaches pedals to its oversized front wheel. In some, the front wheel has **60 spokes** and is **1.5 m** in diameter.

1885: The Rover safety bicycle from Britain has a rear wheel driven by a chain attached to the rider's pedals. It also has rubber tyres. The modern bicycle is born!

2018 A typical bicycle today has brakes on both the front and rear wheels, high-pressure tyres and up to **27 gears** to make pedalling easier or harder.

BIKE SHARE

Bike-sharing schemes have created a new bike boom, especially in cities. Under the schemes, a person can hire a bike for a short period. There are bike-sharing schemes in over **1,000 cities** in **50 countries**, but they are particularly popular in China, France and Spain.

Germany: **12,474**

China: **753,508**

United States: **22,390**

France: **42,930**

Spain: **25,084**

Bike-sharing fleets

FRIENDLIEST BICYCLE COUNTRY

There are around **430 million bicycle owners** in China, but Denmark is considered one of the most bicycle-friendly cities in the world. Over **52%** of people in the Danish capital of Copenhagen use a bicycle to travel to work.

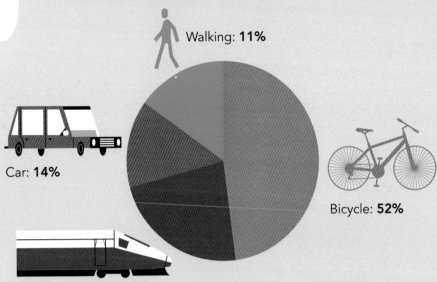

COPENHAGEN COMMUTERS

Walking: **11%**

Car: **14%**

Bicycle: **52%**

Bus, Train, Metro: **23%**

997 km

BIKE LANE CITY

Davis, California, has been named the USA's most bike-friendly city, with **23.3% of daily commutes** made by bicycle. However, the country's city with the highest number of bike lanes is San Diego. Altogether, the distance of San Diego's bike lanes add up to **997 km**.

SMALLEST AND LONGEST

The world's longest bike was made in Australia. It was **41.42 m** long, weighed **2.5 tonnes** and had **20 riders**. However, it still only had **two wheels**! The smallest BMX bike is **3.7 cm high**, **17 cm long** and has **two wheels** the size of large coins.

FURTHER INFORMATION

BOOKS
Machines and Vehicles (The World in Infographics) by Jon Richards and Ed Simkins (Wayland, 2015)
Italian Supercars: Ferrari, Lamborghini, Pagani by Paul Mason (Franklin Watts, 2018)

WEBSITES
A website for kids all about vehicles, from boats and submarines to trains, planes and hot air balloons:
www.sciencekids.co.nz/sciencefacts/vehicles.html
The NASA kids website, with links to games, photos and videos about space vehicles and exploration:
https://spaceplace.nasa.gov/en/search/kids/
A science website for kids about transportation:
http://easyscienceforkids.com/all-about-transportation/

Note to parents and teachers:
Every effort has been made by the publisher to ensure that these websites contain no inappropriate or offensive material. However, because of the nature of the Internet, it is impossible to guarantee that the content of these sites will not be altered. We strongly advise that Internet access is supervised by a responsible adult.

LARGE NUMBERS

1,000,000,000,000,000,000,000,000,000,000,000 = ONE DECILLION

1,000,000,000,000,000,000,000,000,000,000 = ONE NONILLION

1,000,000,000,000,000,000,000,000,000 = ONE OCTILLION

1,000,000,000,000,000,000,000,000 = ONE SEPTILLION

1,000,000,000,000,000,000,000 = ONE SEXTILLION

1,000,000,000,000,000,000 = ONE QUINTILLION

1,000,000,000,000,000 = ONE QUADRILLION

1,000,000,000,000 = ONE TRILLION

1,000,000,000 = ONE BILLION

1,000,000 = ONE MILLION

1000 = ONE THOUSAND

100 = ONE HUNDRED

10 = TEN

1 = ONE

GLOSSARY

astronaut	Someone who trains to travel into space aboard a spacecraft
ballast	A heavy material used to make a ship steady
bulkhead	A wall that separates compartments in a ship's hold
BMX	A heavy-duty bike used for racing around dirt tracks
canal	A man-made waterway used for boats
carbon dioxide	A gas that is breathed out by humans and absorbed by plants
commute	A journey undertaken by workers to get to their jobs
compress	To press something together, often to reduce its size
diesel	A fuel designed for use in vehicles with diesel engines
dinghy	A small boat powered by oars
displace	To move out of position, like a boat moving water
emission	A substance that is released into the air, such as smoke from a chimney
ferry	A boat used to transport passengers and vehicles
fleet	A group of ships
fossil fuel	Fuel such as coal, oil or natural gas that is formed in the Earth from plants and animal remains
gear	A toothed wheel or cog that changes the speed of a vehicle
generator	A machine that changes mechanical energy into electrical energy
gravity	A force that pulls objects towards the surface of a planet, moon or sun
helium	A light, natural gas used for inflating airships and balloons
liner	A ship that is used on a regular line, or route
locomotive	A vehicle such as a train that that uses its machinery to pull something
long-haul truck	A truck that carries cargo over long distances
luxury	Something that is designed to be sumptuous and high-end
magnetism	The way certain metals are attracted to each other
manufacturer	Someone who makes products or goods
merchant	A buyer and seller of goods
metro	A train that operates underground, usually beneath a city
mine	A place underground where minerals, metals or rock are extracted
NASA	The National Aeronautics and Space Administration, the USA's space agency
orbit	The way an object travels around a larger object in space, such as the Earth around the Sun
pollution	Manmade waste which contaminates the environment
port	A place where ships load and unload their cargo
propeller	Blades that turn to move a vehicle such as a ship forward
resurface	To come back onto the water's surface after being beneath it
satellite	An object that stays in orbit around a bigger object in space, such as a space telescope around the Earth
solar power	Electricity that is generated by the Sun, usually via solar panels
submarine	A type of watertight ship that can travel underwater
supersonic	A speed that is faster than the speed of sound
wingspan	The measurement taken across the wings of a bird or aircraft

INDEX

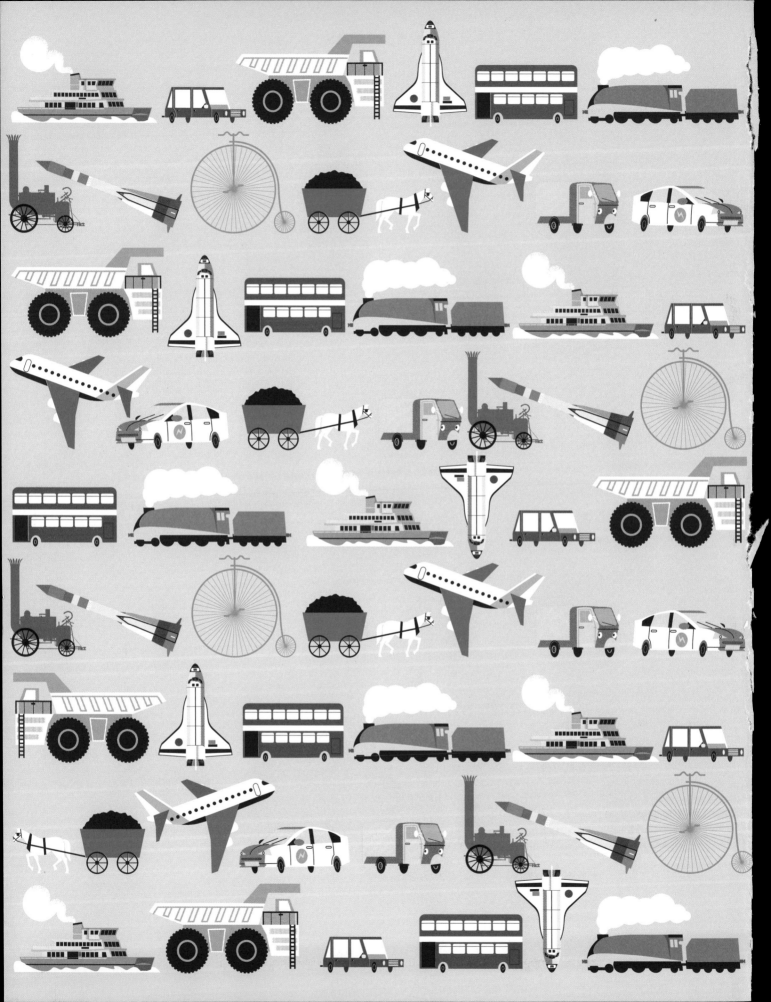